Bigfoot Doesn't Square Dance

There are more books about the Bailey School Kids!
Have you read these adventures?

Bigfoot Doesn't Square Dance

by **Debbie Dadey**
and
Marcia Thornton Jones

illustrated by **John Steven Gurney**

A
LITTLE APPLE
PAPERBACK

SCHOLASTIC INC.
New York   Toronto   London   Auckland   Sydney

ISBN 0-590-84905-0

Text copyright © 1997 by Marcia Thornton Jones and Debra S. Dadey.
Illustrations copyright © 1997 by Scholastic Inc.
All rights reserved. Published by Scholastic Inc.
THE ADVENTURES OF THE BAILEY SCHOOL KIDS in design is a registered trademark of Scholastic Inc.
LITTLE APPLE PAPERBACKS and the LITTLE APPLE PAPERBACKS logo are trademarks of Scholastic Inc.

12 11 10 9 8 7 6 5 4   7 8 9/9 0 1 2/0

Printed in the U.S.A.   40

First Scholastic printing, March 1997

Book design by Laurie Williams

Contents

Bigfoot Doesn't Square Dance

"Maybe if we're lucky we'll see a bear or a deer," Howie said.

Liza looked out the bus window, trying to spot hairy bodies in the dense forest. "Just remember," she told her friends, "don't leave food on the trail."

"We have nothing to worry about from bears," Melody reassured Liza. Melody looked up into the towering pine trees. "Ruby Mountain is as safe as my own backyard."

2

Phe-ew!

"Phe-ew!" Eddie shouted. "What is that disgusting smell?"

Liza held her nose. "Maybe the bus ran over a skunk."

"Either that," Melody said, covering her nose with her pigtails, "or they've turned Ruby Mountain into a garbage heap."

"I always knew this place was a dump," Eddie said.

"Come on," Howie suggested. "Let's get off the bus and out into some fresh air." Howie, Melody, Liza, and Eddie scrambled off the bus behind the other third-graders. But when they got outside, it didn't smell any better.

"I think I'm going to be sick," Liza said when they stood outside the bus. "I've never smelled anything this bad."

"Maybe you should have taken a bath this morning," Eddie teased.

Liza started to argue with Eddie, but she stopped when Mrs. Jeepers looked at them. "Nature is full of peculiar things," she told the students. "Even the smells may seem strange. But to the animals that live here, it is natural."

"That's right," a strange voice said. The Bailey School kids turned to see a woman dressed in a wide-brimmed hat, green shirt tucked into green pants, and hiking boots. A camera hung from a strap slung over her shoulder. "My name is Lily, and I'm the Ruby Mountain park ranger. I'll be guiding your hike today."

"Are you going to take our picture?" Eddie asked. He gave her a toothy grin to show what a good picture he'd take.

The ranger tapped her camera with a fingernail. "I carry this in case I spot an unusual specimen in the wild."

"Eddie's very unusual," Melody giggled.

Eddie reached out to pull Melody's pig-

tails, but decided not to when Mrs. Jeepers touched the brooch at her throat. Then Mrs. Jeepers smiled her odd little half smile. "My students are prepared to experience nature as it was before highways and cities," she told Ranger Lily. "Shall we begin?"

Ranger Lily nodded. "Follow me," she said. "Just remember to stay on the trail and let me know if you see anything . . . strange."

A boy named Huey raised his hand. "What do you mean by strange?"

Ranger Lily glanced toward the thick trees, but then she smiled. "Forget I said anything. I'm sure nothing will bother us."

Then she turned and headed down the narrow trail, leading the third-graders into the shadow of the tall trees. Howie, Liza, Eddie, and Melody stayed together at the back of the line.

Eddie snickered at a few girls who jumped when a bird squawked from a tall tree. "It's like they've never heard a bird before," he told Howie.

"There are some unusual sounds," Liza told him.

"Nothing more than blackbirds and mosquitoes," Eddie said. "And I could see those in my own backyard."

"Then what was that?" Melody asked.

"I didn't hear anything," Howie said.

Melody grabbed his arm and pulled him to a stop. Liza and Eddie ran smack-dab into them.

"What did you do that for?" Eddie asked.

"Shh," Melody warned. "Listen. There's something following us."

"Whatever it is, it stinks," Eddie said as he sniffed. "And it's getting closer."

The four kids stood still, and soon the sounds of the other hikers faded down the trail. That's when they heard it. The thud of heavy footsteps behind them. But when the four friends peered between the trees, they couldn't see anything.

"It sounds big," Melody whispered. "Real big."

"And it sounds like it's following us," Liza whimpered.

Howie swallowed hard. "Maybe we'd better find the ranger. She'll know what it is."

Eddie didn't wait for his friends to answer. He turned and hurried down the trail. Liza, Howie, and Melody raced after him.

3

Be Afraid

Howie, Liza, and Melody caught up with the rest of their class. They kept looking over their shoulders, but they didn't hear the heavy footsteps again. Eddie hung at the back of the group, not paying attention to a thing Ranger Lily said as she pointed out tiny animals. Eddie was too busy looking at the ground.

As soon as they got back to the shelter for lunch, Ranger Lily waved good-bye and started to head back down the trail.

"You cannot stay and picnic with us?" Mrs. Jeepers asked Ranger Lily.

Ranger Lily nervously looked into the shadows of the towering trees. "Thank you, but . . . I've been looking for something. I think I might know where to find it." Then Ranger Lily disappeared, leaving the Bailey School third-graders all alone.

Most of the kids hurried to sit under the shelter and eat their lunches, but not Melody, Liza, Eddie, and Howie. They nibbled their peanut butter sandwiches and pretzels in the shade of a huge hemlock tree.

Howie licked peanut butter off his fingers before poking Eddie on the shoulder. "Why are you acting like somebody just stole the freckles off your face?" he asked Eddie.

"I think that awful nature smell pickled his brains," Melody said with a giggle.

His three friends waited for him to answer. Eddie was famous for his jokes and the tricks he played on people. Usually, he'd do anything to annoy Ranger Lily or get the rest of the kids to misbehave. But ever since the hike, Eddie had been strangely quiet.

Eddie swallowed another bite of his sandwich before answering Howie. "I saw something out there," he said. "And I think we should all be afraid. Very afraid."

"What are you talking about?" Melody asked. "What could there possibly be on Ruby Mountain to be scared of?"

Eddie looked each of his friends in the eyes. Then he whispered his answer. "Bigfoot!" he said.

"Bigfoot?" Melody, Howie, and Liza all gasped at once.

"Shh," warned Eddie, a finger to his lips. "We can't let him hear us."

"Can't let *who* hear us?" Howie asked. "You're not making any sense."

"Bigfoot," Eddie said again. "That's who."

"Bigfoot's a monster that lives in the woods," Melody said.

"Way out near the Pacific Ocean," added Howie.

"Exactly," Eddie said. "Now you see what I mean."

"We don't see anything," Liza told him. "We're not anywhere near the Pacific Ocean and there have never been any monsters hiding in these forests."

"Until now," Eddie whispered, looking over his shoulder.

"The only monster in these woods is you," Howie said.

"Howie's right," Melody said. "You can't be sure there's a monster out there."

"Yes, I can," Eddie said, "because I saw tracks on the trail. Bigfoot tracks!"

Howie smiled. "The only tracks you saw on that trail belonged to the Bailey School kids."

Eddie took a deep breath and nodded. "At first, that's what I thought. But these tracks were huge."

"Then they were made by Ranger Lily," Liza said. "Her boots are big."

"Her hiking boots look like a baby's booties compared to the size of these tracks," Eddie argued. "And whoever made these tracks was barefoot. I saw the toe prints."

Howie slapped his friend on the back. "That explains everything," Howie said. "You probably saw an animal's paw prints."

"It was an animal, all right," Eddie said in his most serious voice. "And that animal was Bigfoot!"

4

Squash

Melody didn't have a chance to argue because just then the tallest, hairiest man she had ever seen in her life lumbered out of the woods. He was at least seven feet tall with a long ponytail hanging down his back and a beard that nearly touched the buckle on his belt. In fact, he had hair everywhere. Even his knuckles looked furry.

"Who's that?" Howie whispered.

Melody shrugged. "Maybe he's another ranger."

"Nice hat," Eddie said with a snicker. The large hairy guy was topped by the biggest hat Eddie had ever seen. It was the kind cowboys wear.

"That's called a ten-gallon hat," Howie explained.

"It looks more like a seven-hundred-and-sixty-five gallon hat to me," Eddie said.

"Those trees are so thick I didn't see him coming," Liza whispered.

"How could we miss him?" Howie asked. "He's as tall as a Christmas tree!" It was true. The man was so tall he had to duck when he walked under a tree.

"He must be from Texas," Liza said softly. "I heard everything is big there. He's so used to ducking, his shoulders are stooped."

"I'll say he's stupid," Eddie muttered.

"You're the stupid one," Liza told him. "I said stooped, not stupid. Like the hunchback of Notre Dame."

Eddie was ready to call Liza stupid plus a few more names, but he didn't get a chance because the stranger walked straight toward them.

The man stopped a few feet away from the four friends. "I overheard your class is interested in what things were like before there were cars and planes," the man growled. "I noticed the ranger slipped back into the woods, so I decided to show your class about life in the Old West. We'll start with dancing."

Liza held up her hand and the big man scowled at her. "What do you want?" he bellowed.

"I was just wondering what your name is," Liza asked.

"Name?" the big man grumbled.

"Yes," Liza said. "What should we call you?"

He rubbed his hairy chin and paused for a moment. The kids stared at each other until the big man answered.

"Squash," he finally growled. "Mr. Squash. Now, get to the shelter. We'll divide into groups."

The kids hurried off toward the open building. Everyone, that is, but Eddie. Eddie stood still, staring at Mr. Squash's back.

"Come on," Howie said to Eddie. "We'll be the last ones."

Eddie didn't say a word. He just kept staring.

"Come on," Howie said again, tugging on Eddie's arm.

Eddie gulped and looked at Howie. "There's something very strange about Mr. Squash," Eddie said.

"I know," Howie said. "He needs to take a bath."

"No," Eddie told his friend. "There's something else."

"What?" Howie said.

"I'm not sure," Eddie said. "But I intend to find out!"

5

Do-si-do

Mr. Squash grabbed a microphone and spoke. His voice echoed down the mountain and halfway to Bailey City. "By the time you leave here," he told the kids, "you'll know how things were in the wild, Wild West before highways and houses covered everything."

A girl named Carey yelled out. Carey's father was the president of Bailey City Bank, and she was used to saying anything she wanted. "My father says highways and houses are good for business."

Mr. Squash frowned at her. "I've never met a wild animal who agreed with your father," he said. Then he turned on a tape player. Fiddle music blasted over the loudspeaker.

"Let's start your Wild West adventure

with a little square dancing," Mr. Squash yelled into the microphone. "Choose a partner and circle 'round."

Melody grabbed Eddie's hand and Howie joined Liza. The rest of the Bailey kids scrambled to get a partner. Then Mr. Squash showed them how to do the promenade and do-si-do.

"Ouch!" Melody yelled when Eddie stepped on her foot.

"I'd much rather be munching grasshoppers," Eddie complained. "Whoever said dancing was fun?"

Mr. Squash gathered the kids in a big circle so he could show them a few more steps. Eddie accidentally kicked Melody when he tried to do the rocky-do, and he missed Liza's hand when they did the grand old right and left.

Mr. Squash swirled Carey around and yelled, "Swing your partner."

Melody hooked arms with Eddie and swung him extra hard. Eddie twirled like a crazed tornado until he bumped into Liza. They both tumbled to the ground.

"My feet are too big for dancing," Eddie said, his face bright red. "Besides, dancing is dumb."

"Dancing is how the pioneers had fun," Howie shouted. "And your feet aren't

nearly as big as Mr. Squash's. If he can dance, so can you."

"Mr. Squash's feet look bigger than Bailey School lunch trays," Melody said.

Eddie glanced down at Mr. Squash's feet. And that's when Eddie fell flat on his behind.

6

Bigfoot on Ruby Mountain

"Don't be mad just because you fell down," Liza told Eddie. "Not everybody is good at dancing." Liza and her friends were sitting under the huge hemlock tree sipping lemonade. Mr. Squash, Mrs. Jeepers, and the rest of the class were in the shelter.

"I'm not mad," Eddie muttered. "And it wasn't the dancing that made me fall."

"Then why did you fall?" Melody asked.

"I fell down because I was scared," he said.

"About what?" Howie giggled. "Having to hold hands with Carey when we danced?"

Eddie rolled his eyes. "That doesn't scare me. It kills me! But that's not what I'm talking about. I'm talking about see-

ing Bigfoot on the dance floor!" Eddie blurted. "And his name is Mr. Squash!"

Melody laughed. "I think all that dancing made you dizzy," she said.

"Eddie must have do-si-doed his brains clear to Bailey City," Liza said with a giggle.

"The girls are right. The only big foot around here is yours," Howie told his friend. "And it's stuck in your mouth. You're just trying to make excuses for not being able to dance."

"Didn't you see his teeth when he smiled?" Eddie asked.

Liza shook her finger at Eddie. "He can't help it if his teeth are yellow," she said. "Maybe he can't afford a dentist."

"Maybe he ate the dentist," Eddie suggested. "Everybody knows Bigfoot has huge yellow choppers. Just like Mr. Squash."

"Maybe," Howie said. "But I'm pretty sure Bigfoot doesn't square dance on Ruby Mountain."

"Howie's right," Melody said. "Mr. Squash may have big feet, but that doesn't make him a monster."

Eddie glanced over at the shelter. Mr. Squash sat in a corner, watching the rest of the kids drink lemonade. "Believe what you want," Eddie told his friends. "But you'll be sorry when Bigfoot dances right over Bailey City!"

7

Wild, Wild West

By the end of the day, the kids were exhausted. Their field trip to Ruby Mountain was almost over. Mrs. Jeepers was taking a head count of her students while Eddie watched Mr. Squash. He was standing under a tree and looking toward the woods as if he'd heard something. Then he darted behind the picnic shelter and disappeared behind a clump of trees.

"Look," Eddie said, poking Howie. "Bigfoot disappeared!"

"He didn't even say good-bye," Howie said.

"Maybe we should go tell him how much fun we had," Liza said. But they didn't have time because just then they

heard Ranger Lily whistling along the trail. She smiled when she saw the third-graders near the picnic shelter.

"I thought you'd be gone by now," she told Mrs. Jeepers.

Mrs. Jeepers smiled her odd little smile. "We were having too much fun learning to square dance, but we are getting on our way now."

"Square dancing is fun," Ranger Lily agreed. "We should do more square dancing on Ruby Mountain." She slipped off her backpack and camera to help a group of third-graders load a cooler onto the bus.

Eddie pointed to Ranger Lily's camera. "Did you find what you were looking for?" Eddie asked.

"No," she said. "But I came close. I know I'm hot on the trail of finding a rare species."

Eddie wanted to ask her more, but Mrs. Jeepers put her hand on his shoulder. He looked down at his teacher's long green fingernails. He backed away, hurrying to join the rest of his friends as they climbed aboard the Bailey School bus.

"I'm tired," Liza complained as they sat down.

"Me, too," Howie said. "But this was a great way to learn about the woods and the wild, Wild West."

Melody nodded. "That Mr. Squash really knows about the old days. I heard him tell Carey that he used to live deep in the mountains on the West Coast."

Eddie plopped down in the seat next to Howie without saying a word. All around them kids dropped their backpacks and settled onto the bus.

"Can I sit by the window?" Liza asked Melody.

"You always get to sit by the window," Melody complained. "Why can't I have a turn?"

"Let her sit by the window so she won't get sick all over me," Eddie muttered.

Melody sighed and let Liza move over to the open window. Liza stared out the window as the bus crunched over the gravel road and slowly pulled away from Ruby Mountain.

They hadn't gone far when Liza sat up straight and screamed, "There's a wild animal out there!"

Melody stood up and stared out the window into the darkening forest. "Was it a coyote?" she asked.

"No," Liza gasped. "It was bigger than a coyote. Much bigger."

"I bet it was a deer," Howie guessed.

Liza shook her head. "It couldn't have been a deer. It had too much hair and it ran on two legs."

"It had to be a bear," Melody decided.

"I don't see anything," Carey said. All the kids peered into the trees. Everybody

but Eddie. He sat quietly in his seat, not even bothering to look.

"Don't you want to see?" Melody asked.

"I don't need to look," Eddie said softly. "I already know what it is!"

8

Operation Eddie

"Something is terribly wrong with Eddie," Melody told Howie and Liza on Saturday. It was the day after their trip to Ruby Mountain and the kids met to play soccer on the school playground. They were in their favorite meeting place, under a big oak tree.

"I always knew something was wrong with Eddie," Howie teased.

"This is serious," Melody told him. "I'm worried about him. I just saw him do something the normal Eddie would never do."

"There is no such thing as a normal Eddie," Liza said.

"This is different." Melody told them. "I just saw Eddie walk into the Bailey City library."

"The library!" Howie and Liza gasped. They knew Eddie. They also knew the last place Eddie would go by himself was the library, especially on Saturday morning.

"It gets worse," Melody said, her forehead wrinkled by a frown.

"What could be worse?" Liza asked.

Melody looked each of her friends in the eyes before answering. When she spoke she sounded serious. Very serious. "He was carrying a stack of books!"

Liza gasped and Howie fell back against the trunk of the giant oak tree. "Eddie must really be sick. Why else would he have a bunch of books?" Liza asked.

"You're right," Howie said. "This is serious. This calls for immediate action. Be prepared for Operation Eddie."

Liza grabbed Howie's arm. "You mean we're going to have to do surgery?" she asked.

"No," Howie snapped. "I mean we're going to spy on him. Eddie's up to something. And with Eddie, it's bound to be no good. We have to stop him."

Liza shook her head. "I don't think friends are supposed to spy on each other," she said. "Why can't we just ask him what's wrong?"

"We can't walk up to Eddie and ask him why he's gone crazy," Melody said. "Spying is the only way to go."

Howie, Melody, and Liza raced across the playground to the library. Quietly, they sneaked past Mr. Cooper, the assistant librarian, and tiptoed into the non-fiction section.

"There's Eddie," Melody whispered. Eddie was sitting at a long wooden table surrounded by big books. Howie, Melody, and Liza ducked behind a shelf as Eddie slammed a book shut. When they peered out again, Eddie had already opened another book.

"I'm going to find out what he's doing," Liza whispered. Before Howie or Melody could stop her, she got down on her hands and knees. Silently, she inched up behind Eddie. She peeked over his shoulder to see what he was reading.

Just as Liza read the title a hand grabbed her shoulder and squeezed hard.

"Ahhh!" Liza screamed.

Eddie fell back in his chair, knocking over the pile of books. When they hit the floor they sounded as loud as Fourth of July fireworks.

"What's going on here?" Mr. Cooper asked, his hand still on Liza's shoulder.

Eddie smiled an innocent smile at Mr. Cooper. "Nothing is going on. I'm just looking at books."

"I don't know what you're up to," Mr. Cooper said, "but I don't want any trouble."

"We'll be good," Liza told him. She hurried to help Eddie pick up his books.

As soon as Mr. Cooper walked away, Melody and Howie came out from their hiding place. Melody snatched Eddie's book. It was called *The Bigfoot Monster*.

"Oh, no," Melody moaned. "You don't really believe this Bigfoot junk?"

"It's not junk," Eddie said, "it's evidence. Bigfoot really exists!"

9

Who You Gonna Call?

Howie ran his hand down a long list of Bigfoot sightings. "Bigfoot has been spotted in nearly every state," Howie said softly.

Eddie nodded. "This book says Bigfoot monsters are searching for new places to live because cities and highways scare them away from their real homes. They're very shy, so they wander the world looking for a quiet mountain to call home."

"Look at this." Melody pointed to a dozen listings. "These aren't far from Bailey City."

"That's right," Eddie said. "Because Bigfoot is living here now."

Liza put her hands on her hips. "Just because Mr. Squash is big and needs to see a dentist, that's no reason to make fun of him."

Eddie shook his head. "I'm not calling him names. I'm just stating a fact. Mr. Squash is Bigfoot."

"You've gone over the edge this time," Melody told Eddie. "Bigfoot is just some made-up creature. I bet these sightings are made-up, too."

Eddie slammed his fist on the table. "All of these people couldn't be making up something like this. And some people are so sure Bigfoot is real they spend their lives searching for him. I read that the first person to get close enough to take a picture of Bigfoot would become rich and famous. There's even a phone number to call if you sight Bigfoot."

"That's the number for crazy people," Howie said softly.

"I'm not crazy," Eddie snapped. "I'll even prove it to you."

Eddie started to read from his book.

"'Bigfoot is very tall with brown or black hair covering his body.'"

"That does sound a little like Mr. Squash," Liza admitted.

Eddie continued reading. "'Bigfoot has a terrible odor, somewhat like a skunk.'"

"We did smell something terrible," Melody reminded them.

"That's not all," Eddie said. "Another common name for Bigfoot is Sasquatch."

"That sounds like Squash," Liza gasped.

"Exactly," Eddie said. "And there's more. This book has pictures of people who have seen Bigfoot."

"Those pictures don't prove a thing," Howie argued.

"They do when you know someone in one of them," Eddie told them. He turned a few pages until he found a fuzzy picture. Then he showed it to his friends. There, in black and white, was Ranger Lily. "She's here in Bailey City to capture Bigfoot."

"I still don't believe it," Melody said. "But even if Bigfoot has moved to Ruby Mountain, what could we do about it? Call Bigfoot Busters?"

"Very funny," Eddie said. "No, there's only one thing we can do." He took a deep breath, then slowly said, "We have to catch Bigfoot!"

10

Catching Bigfoot

"Have you lost your mind?" Melody said as the four friends left the library. "If there really is a Bigfoot, he could bite off our heads and spit them out for target practice."

"It's too dangerous," Liza said, nodding.

"We have to go back to Ruby Mountain," Eddie explained. "It's the only way to prove that Mr. Squash is actually Bigfoot."

Howie shifted from foot to foot. "Listen," Howie said. "I don't think there really is such a thing as Bigfoot, but going back to Ruby Mountain alone is a crazy idea. There may be a bear or some other wild animal hiding in those trees."

Liza's eyes were wide as she nodded. "I

did see something when we were leaving. And it was very big. I bet it was dangerous."

"Not to mention hungry. Whatever it was could roll us in mud and eat us for dessert," Melody said.

Eddie held his backpack up for his friends to see. "I have everything I need to catch Bigfoot right in here."

"What's that?" Howie asked. "An atomic bomb?"

"Ha, ha," Eddie sneered. "I have my dad's camera and it's loaded. We're going to capture Bigfoot on film. We'll be rich and famous!"

"That camera needs to be loaded with extra brains for your head," Melody suggested.

Eddie put on his backpack and looked Melody straight in the eyes. "Didn't you say Ruby Mountain is as safe as your backyard?"

Melody shrugged. "That was before all this talk of Bigfoot monsters."

"And before I saw some wild creature in the woods," Liza told Eddie.

Eddie walked toward the bus stop. "That wild creature is Bigfoot. And to-morrow at about this time, I'm going to be famous. I'm going to be the only kid to ever capture Bigfoot in living color. I'll be in the newspaper and on the news. I bet they even make a movie-of-the-week about me."

Howie walked after Eddie. "You'll be in the paper, all right," Howie said. "The headlines in the paper will read: *Boy and camera eaten by wild animal.*"

"Don't go," Melody warned. "It's too dangerous to go by yourself."

Eddie looked at Melody. "I won't be by myself," he said. "Because you're going with me!"

11

Just Us . . . and Bigfoot

Melody, Liza, Howie, and Eddie stepped off the city bus at the bottom of Ruby Mountain.

"Are you sure you want to get off here?" the bus driver asked. "I won't be back until six o'clock. It'll be getting dark by then."

"Six o'clock is fine," Eddie told the driver. "We're not scared."

The driver shrugged and pulled away. The four kids were left standing on the gravel road leading up Ruby Mountain. Liza jumped when a bird squawked in the woods.

"I don't know how I let you talk me into making this crazy trip," Liza said to Eddie.

"You won't think it's crazy when we're

famous for catching Bigfoot," Eddie said, pulling the camera out of his backpack and putting the strap around his neck. "Come on, let's go up by the shelter."

"That's a pretty fancy camera. Do you even know how to use it?" Howie asked.

Eddie's face got red. "Of course I do. My dad showed me last summer."

The four kids walked up the road and slid in behind some trees across from the shelter to wait for Bigfoot.

They waited and waited. Bees buzzed nearby and mosquitoes started biting. "I'm getting eaten alive by these bugs," Liza complained, squirming around.

"Just be grateful Bigfoot isn't munching on your toes," Melody said.

"Ouch," Liza squealed and jumped in front of Eddie. "Another one bit me."

Eddie put his hand over Liza's mouth. "I'm going to bite you if you're not quiet," he told Liza. "If Bigfoot hears us, we'll never be able to capture him. Just sit down and stay out of my way."

Liza stuck out her tongue at Eddie. She stooped down in front of him and tried to stay still. It wasn't easy. Bugs were everywhere. To top it off, it was getting dark. Liza gulped when a giant spider headed for the toe of her shoe.

"Look," Liza gasped.

Eddie nodded and held up his camera. He was staring beyond the shelter to some trees. A huge hairy shape stood with its back to them. "It's Bigfoot," Eddie whispered. Then he started snapping pictures.

12

Trapped

"Get it off me!" Liza squealed and jumped up from the ground.

"You're in my way," Eddie hissed. He kept snapping pictures while Liza kept squealing.

"Get it off me!" Liza yelled again, wiggling her foot in the air. The hairy spider clung to Liza's white shoe.

"What is wrong with you?" Melody whispered. "Do you want Bigfoot to see us?"

Liza pointed to her shoe. She looked ready to cry. "Get it off before it bites me!"

Melody took one look at the spider and rolled her eyes. Without a word, she flicked the spider off Liza's shoe.

"There, it's gone," Melody said.

"Yeah, it is," Howie agreed. He nodded to the woods where the hairy creature had stood. Now there were only trees.

"Why did you have to make such a fuss about that little spider?" Melody complained to Liza. "You scared off Bigfoot."

"Little spider!" Liza shrieked. "That thing was the size of Michigan."

"That's okay," Eddie said. "One picture is the only proof we need. We'll be famous."

Howie checked his glow-in-the-dark watch. "We'll be late for the bus if we don't hurry," Howie told his friends.

"Come on," Melody said. She raced down the gravel road toward the bus stop. Howie, Eddie, and Liza followed closely behind.

"I bet I have bug bites all over me," Liza complained. "These bugs are terrible."

"Not as terrible as what's behind you," Howie said. All the kids looked over their shoulders. There was Mr. Squash taking

monster steps toward them. He had on his cowboy hat, and he looked mad.

Melody saw the bus first. "Wait!" she screamed. She jumped up and down and waved for the bus to stop. But it was too late. The bus pulled away just as they got to the bottom of the gravel road.

"Oh, no," Liza squealed. "We're trapped on Ruby Mountain!"

"We're dead," Eddie said.

"Not yet," Melody screamed. "RUN!"

13

All the Proof We Need!

Melody, Liza, Howie, and Eddie raced after the bus. "Stop!" they yelled. They rounded a bend in the road and almost ran into the back of the city bus.

"I thought you kids might have high-tailed it back to town without me," the bus driver said as they climbed on. "Lucky for you one of the passengers saw you waving."

Liza panted and collapsed into a seat. "Thanks for stopping," she said.

"You saved our lives!" Howie told the bus driver. Howie looked out the back window and saw Mr. Squash standing in the middle of the road.

The bus roared back down the highway toward Bailey City. Eddie held on tight to his camera, but no one said a word until Mr. Squash and Ruby Mountain were no longer in sight.

The next morning before school the kids met at Dover's Department Store. Eddie flashed an envelope full of pictures he'd just paid for. "This is all the proof we need," Eddie said.

"Let me see," Melody said.

Eddie opened the envelope, but somebody reached over a nearby shelf and grabbed his shoulder.

Eddie peered up into the angry face of Ranger Lily. "The bus driver told me you went to Ruby Mountain. What were you kids doing there all by yourself?" she asked them. "Don't you know it's dangerous? There could be wild animals roaming about."

Eddie pulled away from Ranger Lily and held up the envelope. "We know all about the wild animals there. And we know you're searching for the biggest one of all. But we found him first. We're

going to be famous with these pictures, and Mr. Squash will be history!"

Ranger Lily's forehead crinkled in a worried frown. "Eddie," she said, "I don't know what you're talking about. And I don't have time to figure it out because I have to hire a square-dancing teacher."

"What about Mr. Squash?" Liza asked.

Ranger Lily looked puzzled. "I don't know any squash. The last teacher moved out west two months ago." Eddie looked at his friends and raised his eyebrows. Ranger Lily put her hands on her hips. "I want to make sure you stay away from Ruby Mountain unless you're with an adult. It could be dangerous up there."

Eddie waited until Ranger Lily walked away. He smiled as if he'd just won an Olympic gold medal. "She was looking for Bigfoot, but we found him first. And I have the proof right here."

"Let me see those," Howie said, grabbing the envelope away from Eddie.

Without a word, Howie thumbed through the pictures.

"Can you see Bigfoot?" Melody asked.

Howie shook his head. "They're pictures of a foot, all right. Liza's!"

"What?" Eddie yelled, grabbing the pictures. Eddie looked at the pictures and then looked at Liza. "I told you to stay out of my way," he snapped.

"Oops," Liza said. "I guess the only one with a big foot around Bailey City is me!"

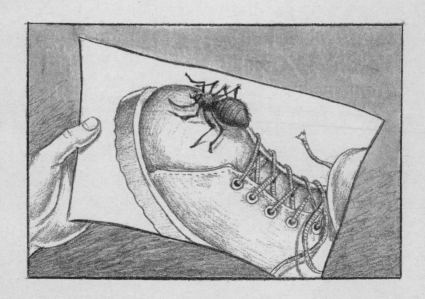

"This proves that there really wasn't a Bigfoot creature on Ruby Mountain," Melody said.

"After all," Liza said with a giggle, "Bigfoot doesn't square dance."

Howie laughed. "And neither does Eddie!"

The Adventures of THE BAILEY SCHOOL KIDS®

Frankenstein Doesn't Plant Petunias, Ghosts Don't Eat Potato Chips, and Aliens Don't Wear Braces ... or do they?

Find out about the creepiest, weirdest, funniest things that happen to The Bailey School Kids!™ Collect and read them all!

LITTLE 🍎 APPLE®

Here are some of our favorite Little Apples.

There are fun times ahead with kids just like you in Little Apple books! Once you take a bite out of a Little Apple—you'll want to read more!

Reading Excitement for Kids with BIG Appetites!

- ☐ NA45899-X **Amber Brown Is Not a Crayon**
  Paula Danziger $2.99
- ☐ NA93425-2 **Amber Brown Goes Fourth**
  Paula Danziger $2.99
- ☐ NA50207-7 **You Can't Eat Your Chicken Pox, Amber Brown**
  Paula Danziger $2.99
- ☐ NA42833-0 **Catwings** Ursula K. LeGuin $2.95
- ☐ NA42832-2 **Catwings Return** Ursula K. LeGuin $3.50
- ☐ NA41821-1 **Class Clown** Johanna Hurwitz $2.99
- ☐ NA42400-9 **Five True Horse Stories**
  Margaret Davidson $2.99
- ☐ NA43868-9 **The Haunting of Grade Three**
  Grace Maccarone $2.99
- ☐ NA40966-2 **Rent a Third Grader** B.B. Hiller $2.99
- ☐ NA41944-7 **The Return of the Third Grade Ghost Hunters**
  Grace Maccarone $2.99
- ☐ NA42031-3 **Teacher's Pet** Johanna Hurwitz $3.50

Available wherever you buy books...or use the coupon below.

SCHOLASTIC INC., P.O. Box 7502, 2931 East McCarty Street, Jefferson City, MO 65102

Please send me the books I have checked above. I am enclosing $ _____ (please add $2.00 to cover shipping and handling). Send check or money order—no cash or C.O.D.s please.

Name_____

Address_____

City_____State/Zip_____

Please allow four to six weeks for delivery. Offer good in the U.S.A. only. Sorry, mail orders are not available to residents of Canada. Prices subject to change.   LA996